PRINCESSES
Wear Pants

SAVANNAH GUTHRIE *and* **ALLISON OPPENHEIM**
Illustrated by **EVA BYRNE**

Abrams Books for Young Readers · New York

For my Vale, who always amazes.
— S. G.

For brave girls with mismatched shoes and glitter in their hair
who build things out of cardboard boxes . . . and the boys who love them.
And to my little royals: Ascher, Ike, and
Princess Rose, who wears whatever she chooses.
— A. O.

The art in this book was created digitally.

Cataloging-in-Publication Data has been applied for
and may be obtained from the Library of Congress.
ISBN: 978-1-4197-2603-3

Text and illustrations copyright © 2017 Savannah Guthrie and Allison Oppenheim
Book design by Pamela Notarantonio

Printed and bound in China
10 9 8 7 6 5 4 3 2

Abrams Books for Young Readers are available at special discounts when
purchased in quantity for premiums and promotions as well as fundraising or
educational use. Special editions can also be created to specification. For details,
contact specialsales@abramsbooks.com or the address below.

ABRAMS The Art of Books
115 West 18th Street, New York, NY 10011
abramsbooks.com

TO ALL WHO CHOOSE TO READ THIS BOOK,
IT'S TIME TO GIVE PRINCESSES A SECOND LOOK!
THE PINEAPPLE KINGDOM HAS A STORY TO SHARE
OF A SPECIAL YOUNG PRINCESS AND A SURPRISING AFFAIR.

Princess Penelope Pineapple
was her name,
With brown eyes, pink cheeks,
and pigtails of fame.

The one thing more admired
than her long flowy tresses
Was her closet full of tiaras
and dazzling dresses.

Penny was the daughter of the king and queen.
Atop Pineapple Castle she could often be seen

With her brother, Philippe, and the royal cat,
"Miss Fussywiggles"—what a silly name is that!

A proper young lady, Penny could paint, sing, and dance . . .

But did you know about her collection of pants?

Crowns and gowns have their place, no doubt.

But that's not *all* this girl was about.

She loved to sparkle, loved ruffles, too.
"But I wear pants," she said, "'cause I've got things to do!"

Early each morning as the sun would rise,
Penny got up to exercise.
She'd pull on her yoga pants and a T-shirt
(Because a workout, of course, is no place for a skirt).

Tending the garden was a very big job,
Growing tomatoes and corn on the cob.
"To feed those in need of a meal is my duty,"
Said the princess in pants, paying no mind to beauty.

A pilot in the Pineapple Air Command,
She did high-flying tricks while guarding the land.

In her sequined flight suit, Penny never was scared.
She flipped and flew higher than others had dared.

And Penny hosted
the Pineapple Science Fair,
A place for kids
with ideas to share.

With solar cars, robots, and cures for the sick,
Her lab coat and corduroys did just the trick.

But sometimes Penny just liked to unwind,
Wearing comfy old jeans, the patched-up kind.
She'd read books, or daydream, or write a long letter
To Great-Grandma Pineapple to make her feel better.

Then came the night of the Pineapple Ball,
The event of the season: "Come one, come all!"
Ladies and gents in their costumes so fine,
Sipping Pineapple Punch. "Oh, how divine!"

Grand Lady Busyboots would surely be there
With her wagging finger and disapproving stare.
"Pants have no place on a lady!" she'd say.
"That's how it has been, and that's how it should stay."

Penny gazed at her gowns all lined up in a row.
"If I can't wear pants, then I don't want to go.
I love to dress up, just as pretty as can be . . .
But underneath it all, I still have to be ME!"

Once at the ball, Penny forgot all her troubles.
The courtyard was brilliant with baubles and bubbles.
As the crowds climbed down the palace staircase,
None could imagine what would soon take place.

For just at that moment, a terrible wail
Came from high above where a long furry tail
Could be seen hanging down from the tower's north wall . . .
It was the royal kitty, trying hard not to fall!

"Miss Fussy!!!" screeched Penny. The music then stopped.
Every eye turned upward, every jaw dropped.
Kerplunk went the cat in the moat down below,
Her royal coat soaked from ear to toe.

Prince Philippe cried out as he fell to his knees.
"She cannot swim! Someone help her, please!

I'd save her myself, but my suit would get wet.
I'm not dressed to rescue the poor royal pet!"

Penny was ready, no need for preparing,
To spring into action, no matter what she was wearing.
The crowd thought for sure in her gown she'd be sunk,
But under her skirts were her pink swimming trunks!

She dived into the water
and swam toward the cat

And rescued Miss Fussy
in five seconds flat!

Miss Fussy in arm, Penny swam back around,
Slipped on her shoes and shook off her gown.

She handed the cat to a grateful Prince P
Who said, "In dresses or trunks, you're braver than me."
The kingdom rejoiced and sang Penny's praises,
"The Pineapple Princess always amazes!"

The Pineapple Kingdom proudly agreed,
"We must be ourselves, as the lady decreed.
The princess helped when no one else could.
She saved the day, just like a good royal should."

Penny smiled and said as she started to dance,
"It's what princesses do. This is why we wear pants!"

Lady Busyboots took the stage and grabbed the mic.
"From now on, princesses should wear whatever they like!
We've all learned a lesson from Penny today.
Sometimes our dresses can get in the way."